Ellie-May & her Toy Dragon, Ben

by Genna Rowbotham ,

For Charlie, Holly, and Beatrice!

Ellie-May & her Toy Dragon, Ben
Written by Genna Rowbotham

A CIP catalogue record for this book is
available from the British Library.
ISBN: 978-1-7398474-6-3

Published in Great Britain 2023
by Adventure Scape Press

Ellie-May & her Toy Dragon, Ben

by Genna Rowbotham

Young Ellie-May
couldn't get to sleep.
She said, "There's no point
in counting sheep."

Feeling so excited
for a new day ahead,
at two in the morning,
she sprang out of bed.

Well, do you know
what Ellie did then?
She stumbled over
her toy dragon, Ben.

"OWW!" she cried,
her eyes red-raw,
for she hadn't slept
the night before.

Then Mummy called out,

"What have you done?"

"I've banged my toe

and fell on my bum."

"It's far too early

to get out of bed!"

Well, do you know

what Ellie-May said?

"I want to run

and I want to play.

I'm so excited

for another day!"

Mummy shook her head
and then left the room.
When suddenly, there was
a great big... BOOM!

What she saw then
was a MASSIVE surprise:
her toy dragon growing
and GROWING in size!

Ben raised his huge head
and then gave a loud, "ROAR!"
"WHOA!" cried Ellie-May,
falling back on the floor.

"Climb upon my back,"
Ben said with a grin.
So, she did; she climbed up
on his red, scaly skin.

"Where are we going?"
she asked gleefully.
"To my castle of course!"
he said joyfully.

"Woo-hoo!" sang Ellie-May.
"Who needs sleep!"
And out through the window,
they both did creep.

Flying up, up and away,
Ben roared, "Hold on tight!"
So, she wrapped her arms around him
with all of her might.

Ellie-May gasped
as the silver moon shone.
But where was her house?
It had already gone.

Ben's SUPER-SIZE wings
flapped higher and higher,
and all of the time,
he breathed flames of fire!

As he stretched his wings wide,
Ben soared past the stars.
Was that planet Venus,
Mercury or Mars?

Maybe it was Mars,

lighting up the night sky,

glowing bright-red

as big Ben flew on by.

Swooping down low
over valleys so deep,
where all the girls and boys
lay fast asleep.

They flew over mountains
and rivers so blue.
It was their little secret
that no one else knew.

Across the blue ocean,
Ben's claws surfed the sea,
where Ellie saw a dolphin
jump up close to her knee.

Ben soared up high again,

so eager to fly,

where even more dragons

coloured the night sky.

"To my castle!" roared Ben,

as he circled down low.

And there on a hill,

was his castle all aglow.

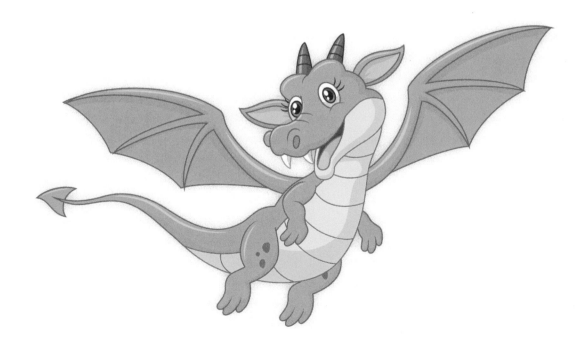

With a great **CRASH** of thunder,

big Ben hit the ground,

as Ellie held on tight

with her head spinning round.

"Welcome to my party!"

Ben heartily said,

as she slid down his tail

rubbing her head.

The brass band played

such a happy, groovy tune,

as the bright stars shone

with the shimmering moon.

They sang and they boogied

until Ellie wandered off,

towards a picnic table

with yummy food to scoff.

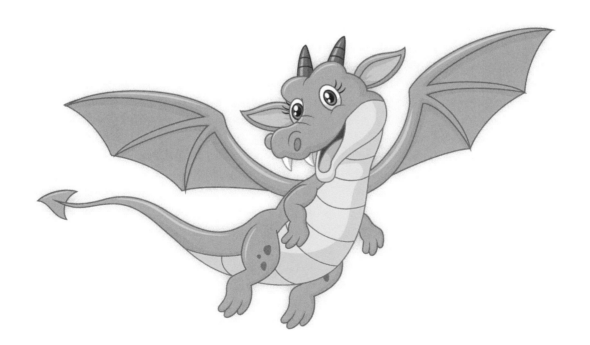

There was dragon-shaped jelly,

party cake and tea.

Ellie-May called out to Ben,

"Come and feast with me!"

So, they had a bit of this,

and a bit of that too.

The best breakfast ever…

If only her mummy knew.

Then she sat on Ben's back,
and they played a fun game:
Ben breathed out grey smoke
until his mouth was aflame!

But then, Ellie felt sick

from the sweets and cream bun,

as the moon waved goodbye

to the bright-yellow sun.

Her eyes began to flicker…

She struggled to see.

Was it the smoke game,

or tiredness maybe?

Screwing her eyes shut,

she rubbed and she rubbed,

'til the tears came,

then she blubbed and she blubbed.

Though she tried not to yawn,

Ellie's mouth opened wide.

Ben wrapped his wings around her,

and she snuggled inside.

"Shall I take you home?"

fiery Ben said.

"Or would you rather

stay – and play instead?"

"Yes," said Ellie-May.
"I'd love to stay and play,
and I'm so excited
for another day.

But first, I need some sleep:
it's important, you know.
It helps me stay healthy
and it helps me to grow!"

So, her friendly dragon, Ben
let out a big, "ROAR!"
Then off, up and away
to the sky, he did soar!

Soon, sleepy Ellie
was flopping into bed,
hugging Ben tightly
as she rested her head.

Lightning Source UK Ltd.
Milton Keynes UK
UKHW051017080123
414947UK00011B/98